ALL THE YEAR ROUND

To our good friend Klaus

First published in 2017 by Andersen Press Ltd., 20 Vauxhall Bridge Road, London SW1V 2SA.

Text copyright © John Yeoman, 2017. Illustration copyright © Quentin Blake, 2017.

The rights of John Yeoman and Quentin Blake to be identified as the author and illustrator of this work

have been asserted by them in accordance with the Copyright, Designs and Patents Act, 1988.

All rights reserved.

First edition.

Printed and bound in Malaysia.

British Library Cataloguing in Publication Data available.

ISBN 978 1 78344 613 1

ALL THE YEAR ROUND

words by John Yeoman

pictures by Quentin Blake

ANDERSEN PRESS

SPRING   SUMMER   AUTUMN   WINTER

There are hundreds of reasons
For welcoming seasons!

JANUARY

"You should wear a thicker sweater." "Take your woolly scarf: it's cold."
Why not put your fur-lined boots on?" Do they think I'm five years old?

I would be a great deal happier if I weren't obliged to wear
All those extra layers like an insulated polar bear.

Wouldn't it be fun to go out, just for once, dressed as I please:

Plastic flip-flops, baggy t-shirt, jeans cut off above the knees.

FEBRUARY

Now and then I get up extra-early, just to make

A super-scrumptious yummy-yummy, light-as-air-type cake.

I weigh and mix and stir and knead, till everything's just so;

The kitchen air is fragrant with the sweetly-smelling dough.

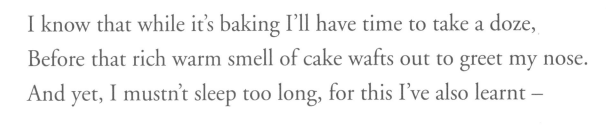

I know that while it's baking I'll have time to take a doze,

Before that rich warm smell of cake wafts out to greet my nose.

And yet, I mustn't sleep too long, for this I've also learnt –

That if I wake to thick black smoke,
it's well and truly burnt!

MARCH

Our group's known for miles around
    For our very special sound.

Haven't got much expertise:
    Often we're in different keys.

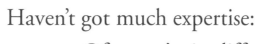

(Paul can only play in F.)

Luckily, we're all tone-deaf.

APRIL

From time to time I feel the urge
          to take a pan and broom
And mop and feather duster,
          and attempt to clean my room.
I empty all the cupboards out
          because I always say
I need to know the things to keep
          and what to throw away.

I spread the stuff across the floor,
          or pile it on the bed:
Those games and toys and t-shirts,
          and those books I've never read.
For hours on end I sort it through,
          without the least success –

For every time I tidy up I make a bigger mess.

MAY

I'm always getting insect bites
    and bruises on the knee;
And grazes on my elbows
    when I climb my favourite tree.

But I can't complain about it
    when I look around and see –

All those many, many others
    who are far worse off than me.

JUNE

Our friends are keen on keeping pets;

        to visit them's a treat.

We watch the creatures groom and climb

        and stretch and drink and eat.

They romp around the room, they yawn,

        they doze – all rolled-up tight –

They twitter, squeal, and growl, and purr –

But, most of all, they bite!

JULY

The sun shining brightly; the shade of a tree.
Just right for a picnic, I think you'll agree.
We whoop with delight as the tablecloth's laid:
We all love the cakes and the cool orangeade,
The eggs and the ham and the pickles and cheese.

And so do the ants and the wasps and the bees!

AUGUST

I found a super bathing-place, concealed among the trees.
In Spring it looks delightful – but the water's fit to freeze.
I use it most in August (there's just me and several sheep)
The water's warm and tempting –

But it's only ankle-deep.

SEPTEMBER

My sister's really hopeless
    when she does her magic show.
She thinks she's reached perfection,
    but she's quite a way to go!

The coin will never reappear
    from underneath the cup;
The strings of flags she pulls
    from sleeves are always tangled up;

The mice she tries to conjure up
    from hats are never there –
They're always running round the room,
    or climbing up your chair.
Her clumsiness at card tricks
    ought to cover her with shame;

But we applaud her dazzling skill at juggling, all the same.

OCTOBER

It's funny how different you look in a cape;
Or stuffed with plump cushions to alter your shape;
Or sporting a jerkin; or top-hat and beard.
Except for my brother –

He always looks weird.

NOVEMBER

It's cold outside, but warm indoors, and we have all we need –
We pile up on the sofa and we settle down to read.
What's it to be? Some wizardry? Or medieval knights?
Or something about ponies? Or interstellar flights?
A wild romantic tale for me, a beast in space for Jim,

While Andy hugs a picture book that's twice as big as him.

DECEMBER

Do not disturb.
Don't knock or ring.
I'm staying here –

Until it's SPRING!